Princess Dinosaur

By Jill Kastner

GREENWILLOW BOOKS
An Imprint of HarperCollinsPublishers

For Carson

Princess Dinosaur
Copyright © 2001 by Jill Kastner
All rights reserved. Printed in Singapore by Tien Wah Press.
www.harperchildrens.com

Watercolors and pen and ink were used for the full-color art.
The text type is Futura Heavy.

with special thanks to Jamie Ransome

Library of Congress Cataloging-in-Publication Data
Kastner, Jill.
Princess Dinosaur / by Jill Kastner.
  p.   cm.
"Greenwillow Books."
Summary: Princess Dinosaur has fun playing with the rest of
the toys until Spots the dog comes and carries her off to an
outdoor adventure.
ISBN 0-688-17045-5 (trade). ISBN 0-688-17046-3 (lib. bdg.)
[1. Toys—Fiction. 2. Dinosaurs—Fiction. 3. Dogs—Fiction.]
I. Title.   PZ7.K1563 Pr 2001   [E]—dc21   00-057305

1 2 3 4 5 6 7 8 9 10 First Edition

Princess Dinosaur wakes up from her nap, refreshed, and looks for something fun to do.

She sees her friend Cowboy Tex
and his pals rustling cattle.
Princess Dinosaur decides
to surprise them.

"Time for an ambush!" She giggles.

In all the ruckus Princess Dinosaur
accidentally takes a bite out of
Cowboy Gus's hat.
Blue Feather's bow is bent, too.

"We're not playing with you anymore!"
Cowboy Gus cries. "You're too rough!"

"Come play with me," calls
Bettina Esmerelda Louise.
They play dress-up.

Princess Dinosaur
tries on some shoes
and a new hat.

Then they have a tea party.

Princess Dinosaur feels restless.

She stands on her head.

She does a cartwheel.

"Watch me jump
on one foot
and then the other!"
she yells.

"All aboard!" The train whistle hoots.
"Let's go for a ride!"
Everyone piles in.

"Story time!" Princess Dinosaur announces at the end of the trip. "Sit down and I'll read you *Goldilocks and the Three Bears.*"

"Oh, no!" cries Duckie.
"Here comes Spots!"

"Quick!" Princess Dinosaur yells.
"Run for the toy box."
Princess Dinosaur helps
Turtle jump in just in time.

But Spots snaps up
Princess Dinosaur
in his jaws and
won't let her go.

Spots carries Princess Dinosaur outside.
"Put me down!" she scolds him.
Spots does put Princess Dinosaur down.

And then he covers her with dirt.
It's so dark she can't see a thing.

Luckily, Princess Dinosaur has long,
sharp, pointy claws.
She digs herself out of Spots's hole
in no time.

Princess Dinosaur brushes the dirt off her skirt
and looks around. She sees somebody. He has
claws and teeth just like hers. He starts to run.
Is this a game?
Should Princess Dinosaur chase him?

No!
Spots is chasing
him already!

Quick!

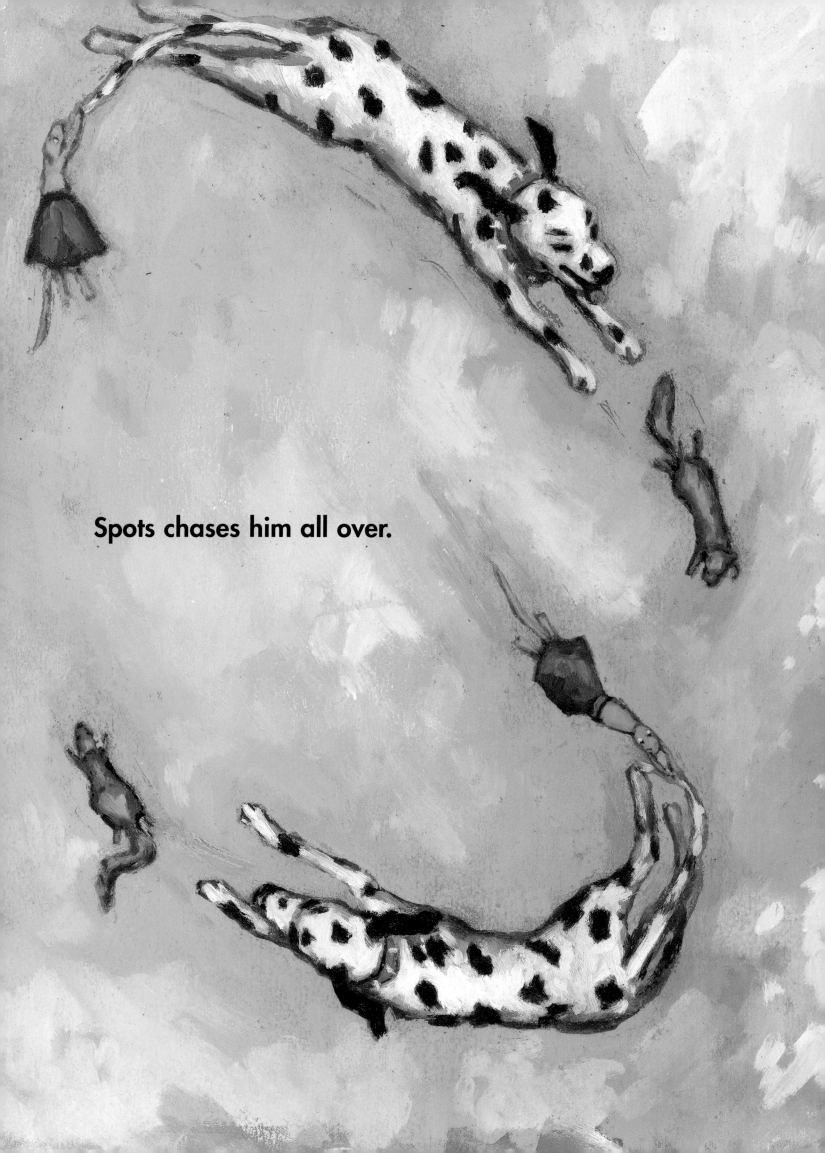

Spots chases him all over.

Spots chases him up a tree.

Then Spots hears
his dinner being opened.

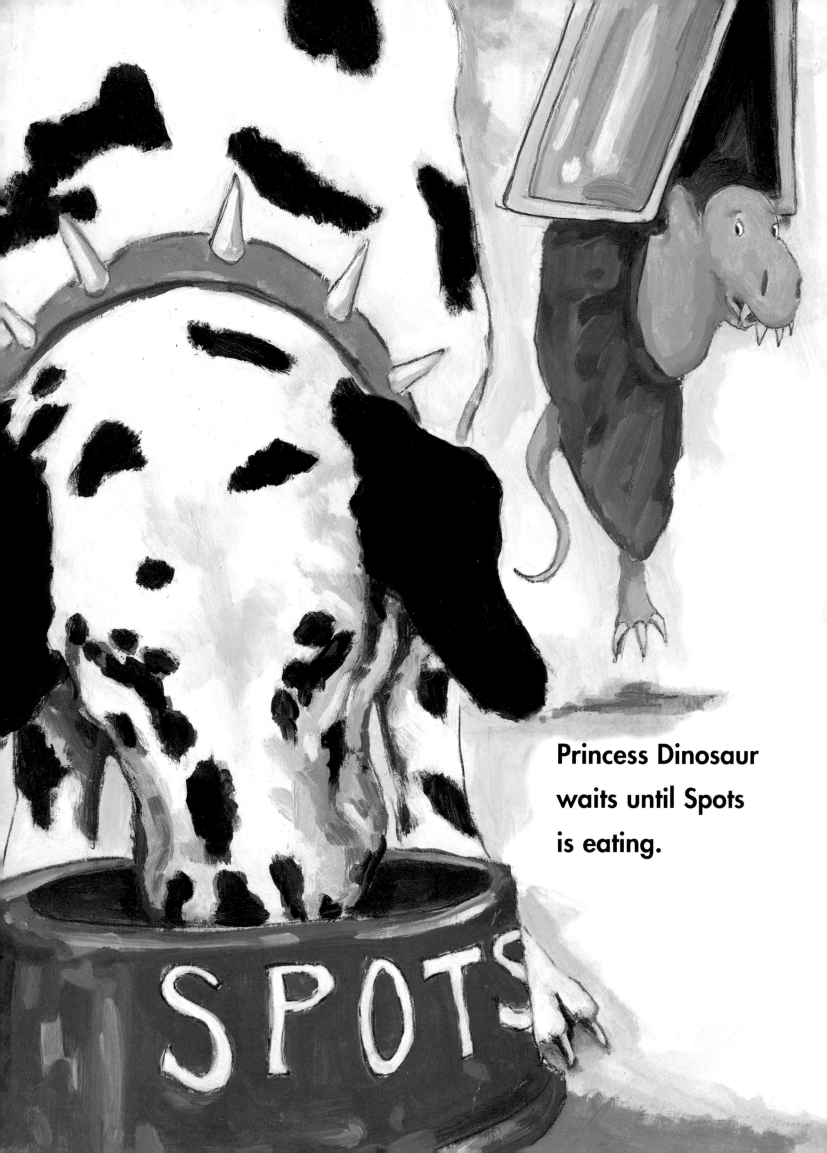

Princess Dinosaur
waits until Spots
is eating.

"You can make it, Princess Dinosaur!" her friends call.

Home again.

THE END